Pearl's Dressing-Up Dreams

The Red Cloak

The Satin Dress
The Diamond Tiara
The Velvet Cloak
The Glass Slippers

The Silver Mirror
The Flowered Apron
The Pearly Comb
The Lace Gown

The Red Cloak
The Party Frock
The Picnic Basket
The Frilly Nightdress

Pearl's Dressing-Up Dreams

The Red Cloak

JENNY OLDFIELD

Illustrated by Dawn Apperley

Hodder
Children's
Books

A division of Hachette Children's Books

Hodder Children's Books
A division of Hachette Children's Books
338 Euston Rd, London NW1 3BH
An Hachette UK company
www.hachette.co.uk

1

"Go downstairs and play while the cake bakes in the oven," Amber's mum said.

"Can't we stay in the kitchen?" Lily asked. She loved the smell of hot cake.

Amber scraped the bowl with a wooden spoon. "Yum!"

"No, let's go." Pearl led the way down to the basement. "Let's play dressing up."

"Boring!" Amber complained. "We

played it yesterday and the day before that."

"Yes, and I'm still waiting to be magicked," Pearl sighed. "It's all right for you and Lily – you've both been whooshed off already."

"Maybe the box has run out of magic clothes." Lily opened the lid. She picked out a pair of red wooden clogs, put them on and began to tap dance on the stone floor. *Clatter-clatter.*

"Hey, here's my fancy dress costume for a party I went to ages ago!" Amber lifted a striped all-in-one suit out of the box. She swished its long striped tail. "And here's the mask. I went as a cat – miaow!"

"What can I wear?" Pearl wondered, pushing her fringe back from her forehead and digging deep into the box. "I've tried the fairy wings and the witch's hat, but they didn't whoosh me."

"Maybe you're wishing too hard for it to happen," Lily suggested. "Try on this piece of raggedy stuff I brought back from Snow-White world instead."

Pearl took the scruffy red shawl from Lily and wrapped it round her shoulders. Then she put on a long flowery skirt.

"And these red clogs." Lily kicked off the shoes and Pearl stepped into them.

"Who am I supposed to be?" Pearl asked as she glanced in the mirror.

"Gretel in 'Hansel and Gretel'," Amber's mum suggested as she came down the stairs with drinks of orange juice and wedges of ginger cake fresh from the oven.

"You look very sweet, Pearl."

"Thanks," Pearl blushed.

"Have fun," Amber's mum called, taking the empty tray back upstairs.

"Gretel got eaten by the wicked witch," Lily whispered, her eyes round and fake-scared. "She got pushed in the oven and baked!"

Amber giggled. "You don't want to be her, Pearl. Anyone but Gretel!"

"Well, I'm not her – I'm not anyone!" Pearl said with a frown. She'd twirled in front of the mirror and done her best to be magicked, but it still wasn't happening.

So she took a big bite of scrummy cake.

"Uh-oh!" Amber saw Pearl bite the cake and go back to her twirling. Suddenly a warm wind blew into the

room and the light grew brighter.

Clickety-clack went Pearl's clogs across the floor. *Twirl-twirl. Munch-munch.*

"Yippee, I'm dizzy!" she cried.

"Stop twirling!" Lily yelled above the din of the wooden shoes. "Pearl, if you're Gretel, you really don't want to go there!"

The light began to dazzle the three girls, silver specks of glitter whirled in on the wind.

"It's happening!" Pearl cried as she felt herself rise from the floor and get wafted higher and higher – out of the room, carried on a silver cloud into a world of magic.

"Come back!" Amber and Lily pleaded.

"No way!" Pearl called from the middle of her bright, glittery cloud. "It's my turn to be magicked – at last!"

"Gretel!" Amber muttered as the silver cloud vanished and took Pearl with it. "She gets dumped in the forest."

"There's a gingerbread house," Lily said. "The witch uses it to tempt Hansel and Gretel inside. She's got red eyes."

"Who?" Amber said with a shudder.

"The witch. Red eyes. She eats people."

"Oh, that's so-o-o not good!" Amber groaned. "Now I'm scared for Pearl – I really am!"

Pearl nearly lost her shawl as the magic wind whirled her down to the ground. She grabbed it just in time and wrapped it tight round her shoulders, waiting for the bright light to stop dazzling her.

"Biddy? Where are you?" A woman stood in a cottage doorway calling her daughter's name. "I've baked your grandmother's favourite – a custard pie!"

Pearl landed in the middle of a green meadow beside a sparkling river. Tall white daisies grew along the banks.

"Bi-i-iddy!" the voice called.

"What's up, Biddy? Have you gone deaf

all of a sudden?" asked a boy fishing in the river. His hair was fair and curly, and he was wearing leather shorts with a bib and braces. "Didn't you hear your ma call?"

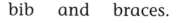

"Are you talking to me?" Pearl said with a frown.

"Yes, of course I'm talking to you. Biddy – that's your name, isn't it?"

"Is it?" Pearl glanced around. She saw a cluster of thatched houses nestled by the edge of the meadow and a small church with a wooden steeple.

"Well, it was Biddy yesterday, and I

12

reckon it's Biddy today and will be tomorrow," the boy grinned. A fish bit at his line and he yanked it out of the water. It wriggled and flip-flopped as he dropped it into his net. "Supper for Dad and me!" he announced cheerfully.

"Biddy, come quickly!" the woman in the doorway called.

"So my name's not Gretel?" she double-checked with the boy, who gave her a long, weird look. "OK, so it's not!" she gabbled, tucking up her long skirt and running towards the cottage. "Anyway, that's a relief!"

Biddy – what kind of silly name is that?
Pearl thought.

She went into the cottage and saw a warm stove and shelves stacked with pots and pans, a kitchen table and pretty jug of flowers on the bright checked tablecloth.

Why not Petronella or Seraphina – something fancy instead of plain old Biddy?

"I want you to carry this basket carefully," Biddy's mother explained. "I'm wrapping the custard pie in a clean napkin and will put in a small pot of butter. Your grandmother likes the butter from our Daisy better than any cow in the valley. Be sure to tell her it was Daisy who gave the milk."

Or Beauty as in "Sleeping Beauty" – a princess, or at least a rich person's daughter. OK, so the cottage was cosy, but this stuff about butter and custard pies wasn't what you expected when you got magicked into a fairy tale.

"Biddy, are you listening to me?" Her mother interrupted her thoughts. "I want you to look after the baby while I finish packing this basket."

15

"The baby?" Pearl looked around until she spotted a wooden cradle by the window.

"Yes, Tommy has just woken up. Will you pick him up and sit with him by the door? Sing him a song."

Whoa! Never in her life had Pearl lifted a baby out of its cot. In fact, she hardly knew one end from another!

"What a dull girl you are today, Biddy!" Bustling across the room, her mother lifted Tommy and dumped him in Pearl's arms. "Outside!" she ordered. "He needs some fresh air."

"Waaagh!" Tommy wailed as soon as Pearl held him. He screwed up his fat pink face, opened his mouth and bawled.

"Shush!" Pearl pleaded. She gave the

16

baby a half-hearted cuddle and found he
was wet at both ends. *Yuck!*

"Sing to him," his mother suggested
from inside the cottage.

"La-la-la!" Pearl warbled.

"Waaagh!" Tommy screamed.

"Ha-ha! He's not keen on your singing,
and I don't blame him. A crow can sing
better than you!" The boy by the river
strode by with his catch. He carried his rod
and net over his shoulder and whistled as
he walked.

"And I'm not keen on your trousers!" Pearl muttered. Silly leather shorts with braces! Where on earth was she? And what was happening?

"I heard that!" The boy winked then vanished through the door of the neighbouring cottage.

"La-la!" Pearl tried again. She sat on a stool and bounced Tommy on her lap.

"Aagh-aagh-aagh!" Tommy cried.

"Here – give him to me." The boy from next door quickly reappeared. He snatched the baby and sat him on his knee. "'This little piggy went to market,'" he began, twitching the baby's big toe. "'This little piggy stayed at home!'"

Tommy stopped bawling and began to smile.

18

"'This little piggy had roast beef, And this little piggy had none!'"

Delighted, Tommy clapped his podgy hands.

"'And this *little* piggy ran wee-wee-wee – all the way home!'"

Tickle-tickle under his chin. The baby chuckled and chortled.

"Huh!" Pearl grunted.

"Your turn," the boy told her as he handed Tommy back.

Just then Biddy's mother came outside with the basket of food. "Ah, Hans, how are you today?" she asked cheerfully.

"Hungry," he said, eyeing the basket.

"And cheeky as ever," Biddy's mum laughed. "Come inside and see what's left over. Maybe a slice of freshly-baked bread

19

would fill that hole in your stomach!"

Everything's about food here! Pearl sighed, sitting on the stool again and praying that Tommy stayed quiet. *It's so not fair. Why isn't it about getting dressed up in jewels and a beautiful satin gown then dancing with a handsome prince, like it was for Amber and Lily?*

Talking about beautiful gowns . . . who was this woman riding into the village on a white horse, surrounded by half a dozen

handsome young riders in shiny purple tunics with gold braid?

All along the street, the blacksmith and the bootmaker, the dairymaid and the farmer's wife bowed low and curtseyed to the lady on the white horse.

She sat side-saddle in a dress of rich purple. Her fair hair was braided and wound around her head like a crown. She wore dainty boots of purple leather

and a velvet cloak hung from her slender shoulders.

Dazzled by her beauty, Pearl forgot to curtsey.

"Quick – come inside!" Hans reached a hand through the doorway and tried to yank Pearl back out of sight.

But it was too late – the purple lady had spotted Pearl and baby Tommy.

"Stop!" she commanded.

The riders came to a halt outside the door of the humble cottage. They sat to attention, staring straight ahead.

The lady stared down at Pearl. "How did you make your baby smile?" she demanded.

"Erm – I didn't – he isn't – I don't know!" Pearl gabbled helplessly.

"The baby is smiling!" the grand lady insisted sharply in her haughty voice. "He is pink and cheerful."

No thanks to me, Pearl thought.

"I have a child who never smiles," the lady went on. "He lies in his golden cradle and he is pale and sad."

Burp! Tommy brought up wind then chuckled in surprise.

"What is your name?" the lady asked Pearl.

"Biddy, your – er – Majest—"

"Your Grace," one of the riders cut across Pearl to correct her. "And you must curtsey to the Duchess each time you speak."

Pearl curtseyed and dreaded what might come next. *Like, "Off with her head!"*

End of story. That would be just my luck, she thought.

"Come to the castle tomorrow," the purple lady ordered. "From henceforth you will be my nursery maid and you will look after my child. You will make him smile."

And without waiting for Pearl's reply, she rode on.

3

"Boo-hoo, poor you!" Hans told Pearl. "I'd rather be eaten by a lion or trampled by an elephant than go to work for the Duchess."

"Why, what's wrong with her?" Pearl asked, jiggling Tommy on her hip.

"Everything."

"Such as?"

Hans stuck his thumbs through his

leather braces and frowned. "Biddy, you know as well as I do that the Duchess is meaner than a snake and twice as sly. Why, it's said she eats servants for breakfast!"

Pearl bit her lip and tried not to think of wicked witches shoving children into ovens. "She doesn't look too bad."

"Ah, but she is." As Tommy began to whimper, Hans took him and spun him round. "Whee!" he cried. "Remember last week when she sent out an order for the mothers in the village to go up to the castle and sing lullabies to her son to send him to sleep?"

"No. What happened?"

"The mothers sang 'Rock-a-bye Baby' until they were blue in the face but none

26

succeeded. The baby never slept a wink. So the Duchess had the mothers kicked downstairs."

"Ouch!"

Hans nodded. "That's why I told you to hide when I saw she was riding by. But you were slower than a tortoise."

"And now I have to work for her," Pearl sighed.

"As a nursery maid," Hans grinned, handing Tommy back to Pearl after he'd finished spinning him round. "Watch out, he's going to be sick!"

Pearl gasped and held the baby at arm's length.

"Only kidding!" Hans grinned.

Pearl grimaced. "Thanks! You know something – I don't even like babies."

"Don't be silly, Biddy. You love little Tommy!" Biddy's plump mum bustled out of the cottage and carried the baby in for his dinner. "Now take the basket to your grandma's house quick as you can, before the butter melts in the sun!"

"So who am I? Where am I? And what happens next?" Pearl walked slowly along the path by the river. Ahead lay a stile leading into a wood. "Do I get a fairy godmother in this story, or what?"

In the bushes by the water's edge, a pair of yellow eyes watched her every move.

"More to the point, where does my grandmother live?" Pearl had carried the basket across the meadow, trying to look like a girl who knew the way to her

28

grandmother's house. But now that she was out of sight of the village, she sat down on the ground and sighed.

"I can't ask the way, even if there was someone around." And there wasn't – not a single person along the riverbank, or on the edge of the wood. Only brown cows grazing in the long meadow. And a bird or two flitting between the tree branches, and perhaps a glimpse of a red squirrel.

The yellow eyes in the bushes blinked then stared again.

Pearl stood up. "Don't be such a wimp," she told herself. "Just go ahead and see where the path leads." Carrying the basket over her arm, she went steadfastly on her way.

But it turned out there was more than one path through the wood.

Pearl climbed the stile and entered the shadow of the tall oak trees. "Huh!" she said, seeing one path to the left, one straight ahead and one to the right.

"Straight ahead!" She decided on the broadest track. Horses had passed this way and left hoofprints. This was definitely the path to take.

So Pearl stepped boldly through the

wood, trying not to mind the shadows and twisted roots, la-la-ing to herself to keep her spirits up.

A twig cracked in the undergrowth. Pearl stopped and looked over her shoulder.

"La-la-la!" she sang in a quavery voice, turning to follow the path again. She didn't mind admitting it – she didn't like this wood. And with each step it grew lonelier, darker . . . and scarier!

"Whoo-whoo!" An owl flapped down from a branch and flew so close that its wings almost brushed Pearl's cheek.

Snap! Another twig cracked.

Toc-toc-toc! A strange sound came from the middle of the wood – a sharp knocking, three tocs at a time . . . silence

. . . then three more tocs.

Pearl stopped dead in her tracks. "What on earth was that?"

Toc-toc-toc . . . Toc-toc-toc. Pearl thought she recognised the sound – it was someone chopping wood!

Without stopping to think, she left the path and ran towards the sound. Behind her, the creature with yellow eyes followed her on soft, padded paws.

"Hey!" Pearl cried as soon as she saw the woodcutter in the clearing ahead. "Can you help me find my way?"

The man stood up and rested against the long handle of his axe. He wore a brown leather tunic and brown boots, and a hat with a speckled feather sticking up from its brim. "Why, Biddy!" he smiled when he saw Pearl running towards him. "What brings you off the path, so deep into the wood?"

"I – I must have got lost!" Pearl gasped. "I'm supposed to be taking this basket of food to my grandmother's house."

"But you started daydreaming as usual, I suppose." Laughing, the woodcutter raised his axe above his head and brought its blade down, deep into a log. All around lay new splinters of wood and to one side a neat pile of firewood.

"Come with me – I'll set you back on the right path."

Phew – this is a piece of luck! Gladly Pearl ran to keep up with the woodcutter's long stride.

"Come on, Biddy – this is the path. Do

you recognise it now?"

Stopping for breath, Pearl saw that they had come to a place at the far edge of the wood.

"See – there is the mill by the river, and beyond that your grandmamma's cottage." The woodcutter gave Pearl a puzzled smile. "I'm surprised that you lost the path, since you come this way almost every day."

"Me too!" Pearl nodded. "Like you say, I must have been daydreaming."

"Well, make sure to stay alert on your way back home," he said. "Remember, the wood can be dangerous."

"It can?" Pearl glanced back into the deep shadows.

"When the Wolf comes down from the

34

mountains into the valley in search of food, he hides here. You must keep your wits about you."

From deep in the undergrowth, the creature with the yellow eyes put out his tongue and drew it slowly across his sharp teeth.

"Yes, I'll remember!" Pearl assured the woodcutter. "And thanks for bringing me this far." She turned towards the mill with its big canvas sails. "Now I have to run. Bye!"

4

"Wrrraaah!" Hans leaped out from behind a bush and scared Pearl out of her wits.

"Aagh!" She dropped the basket.

"Fooled you!" Hans laughed, pawing the air like an angry wolf.

"What are you doing here?" Pearl demanded, falling on to her knees to retrieve the custard pie.

"I came to find Dad and tell him supper was ready. Then I saw you, dithering and daydreaming." Hans folded his arms. "You're such a little simpleton!"

"No I'm not!" Pearl stuffed the pie back into the basket. The mill was only a few steps away and she was anxious to reach her grandma's house. "You're so *not* funny – you know that!"

Hans grinned. "Wraah!"

"Go away!" She waited for him to trot off back to rejoin his dad before she walked on. "And this is not fun either!" she muttered, passing under the creaking sails of the tall wooden windmill. "Getting lost. Getting hauled off to the castle to work for a mean duchess. Not even knowing who I am!"

From a safe distance, the yellow eyes watched and the pink tongue licked its lips.

"Miaow!" A striped cat padded up and rubbed against Pearl's legs. "Miaow! Miaow!"

Pearl bent down to stroke the cat. "Well, at least you seem to know me."

"Tilly-Tilly-Tilly!" A voice as loud as a church bell rang out and an old woman

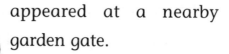

appeared at a nearby garden gate.

The cat peered out from under Pearl's flowery skirt. "Miaow!"

"Ah, there you are!" the old woman cried. "And here you are too, Biddy!

38

Come and give your grandmamma a hug!"

"Pass the jam. Pour the tea. Sit here by the fire." Biddy's grandmother didn't pause for breath. She whizzed around her kitchen fetching plates, buttering scones and gossiping.

Pearl did as she was told. This was one busy kitchen! Scores of jars of blackberry jam were stacked in neat rows on a shelf. Pans bubbled on the stove. Delicious smells wafted out of the oven. "So your mother thought I would enjoy a fresh custard pie, eh, Biddy?" the rosy old woman asked. She was as broad as she was tall, wearing a huge white apron. Taking the pie from the basket, she

gazed at the broken pieces.

"Oops!" Pearl said. Just wait until she saw Hans!

"Never mind – Tilly loves custard." Her grandmother put the pie into a dish and gave it to the cat.

"Miaow!" Tilly agreed.

"Mum said to be sure to tell you that the butter is made from milk taken from Daisy," Pearl told her grandmother.

"My favourite!" Grandmamma said. "Bless your mother – she never forgets what I like. And you too, Biddy. You're a dutiful child, whatever people may say about you."

"What *do* they say?" Pearl felt her cheeks grow red from the heat of the fire. Her plate was stacked with warm scones, jam and cream.

"Why, that you live in a world of your own, my dear. The schoolmistress tells me you're a daydreamer. Everyone knows that you go along with your head in the clouds, dreaming of being a princess!"

"Well, who knows? Maybe I will be," Pearl mumbled through a mouthful of warm jam and scone. It had happened to Amber and Lily. Why shouldn't it happen to her?

41

"That's what I tell people," Grandmamma said, leaning forward. "I tell them that my little Biddy is pretty as the flowers in the meadow, that her hair is like silk. Who knows but that one day a prince may ride by and claim her!"

"Exactly!" Pearl said with a satisfied nod. "Anyway, Grandmamma, I've got some news."

The old woman's eyes lit up. "Let me guess. Is it about Gretchen the milkmaid and my neighbour, Miller Brown?"

"No."

"Or about Farmer Meade's new dairy cow? Lydia East's lost glove? The missing scythe from Ploughman John's hay barn?"

"No, no and no. It's about me," Pearl

42

announced, thinking that here at least was one person who would be pleased. "The Duchess wants me to work at the castle."

It was as if Pearl had said she'd won the lottery. The old woman jumped up from her chair and clasped her hands together. "Oh my! The Duchess – the castle! I can scarcely believe it!"

"It's good, isn't it?"

"Won-der-ful! They say the castle is crammed to the ceilings with rich, handsome young men – guests of the Duke and Duchess. And the ladies dress so finely! Oh my dear, Biddy, are you to be a lady's maid?"

"No. Actually, I have to look after the baby," Pearl admitted.

For a moment her grandmother's face fell. But she soon recovered. "Even so, the baby is of noble birth. And the fine gentlemen will see you come and go. They will stop in the corridors and ask, 'Who is the charming girl with the shining auburn hair?' They will ask your name and you will drop a sweet curtsey."

This all sounded fine to Pearl. It seemed to be her best chance of being a princess after all. "I have to go," she said, looking out at the fading light.

"Yes, you must be sure to reach home before nightfall. But wait, my dear!" Running from the kitchen, the old lady climbed the wooden stairs and opened a large chest in her bedroom. She came back carrying a cloak made of soft red wool. "This is for you, Biddy."

Pearl ran her fingers over the cloak. "Where did you get it from?" she asked.

"It is a cloak I wore for riding when I was a girl," her grandmother explained as she wrapped the garment around Pearl's shoulders. "It was made by the best seamstress out of the finest material. See the hood – it is lined with fur."

"And why do you want me to have it?" Pearl asked, feeling the weight of the cloak and pulling the hood up over her head.

"For you to wear in the cold mornings, and to wrap around yourself on your way home from work. It is a fine cloak. Even the ladies at the castle will envy you and want one of their own."

A red cloak with a hood. Scary rumours about wolves. And a grandmamma. *Aha!* Pearl thought. Her heart gave a sudden jerk and a thud.

"Now take off that shabby old shawl and put the cloak on!" The old woman clapped her hands with delight as she stared at Pearl in the long red cloak. "You look lovely, my dear. From now on you will have a new name to go by, and that name will be Little Red Riding-Hood!"

46

5

So I don't get to be a princess, Pearl sighed as she sped through the wood. The sun had sunk and the moon had risen. There were no princesses in 'Little Red Riding-Hood' – just lots of scary stuff about Mister Wolf.

A shadowy shape loped between the dark trees, its yellow eyes glinting.

Pearl didn't see it. But she felt her heart pound.

And here came the owl again, whoo-whooing past her, swooping so close that she put a hand up to protect her face. "Look behind you-oo-oo!" A voice seemed to hoot a clear message.

"Did that owl just speak?" Pearl said out loud.

A rabbit sat on the path ahead. She twitched her long ears and whiskers, waiting for Pearl. "Why are you out in the wood so late?" the small creature whispered.

"Oh!" Pearl gasped. She stared back but didn't answer.

"There are many dangers. Oh my whiskers, I must run!" The rabbit turned and bobbed out of sight.

"Stop! Look behind you-oo!" the owl

hooted again as he flew back.

Pearl shook her head. This couldn't be happening!

"Do-oo-oo as I say!" the owl hooted.

So Pearl stopped and glanced back the way she had come. She saw only the moon glinting through the branches. Nothing else – except maybe a yellow glint in the undergrowth.

The creature blinked and lay low. He

would bide his time – wait until Pearl came to the deepest part of the wood. Then he would pounce.

Pearl shuddered, gathered her red cloak around her and hurried on.

Now it was really dark – the trees grew so thick and low that she could hardly see the path and she began to stumble.

"What do you get when you pour boiling water down a rabbit hole?" a cheery voice asked. It came from the shadows to one side of the path.

The creature heard footsteps and gave a low growl. *Tomorrow!* he decided. *I will follow Little Red Riding-Hood wherever she goes. And when I find her alone, I will seize my chance!* Then he turned with an empty stomach and slunk away.

"I don't know, son. What do you get when you pour hot water down a rabbit hole?"

"Hot cross bunnies!" Hans declared, bursting into view with his bundle of firewood and spotting Pearl. "It's a joke!" he told her.

"I know it's a joke. It's so not funny!" Pearl didn't let on how glad she was to see Hans and his father.

"Dad, look – it's Biddy, up to no good as usual."

"Well, I hardly recognised you in your fine new cloak!" the woodcutter told her, adjusting the bundle of wood on his broad back. "I see you didn't heed my warning about being out in the wood after dark."

"I couldn't help it. Grandmamma

talked on and on. I couldn't get away."

Hans's dad smiled. "Ah yes. Your grandmother can spin a yarn better than most. And she's in fine voice for a woman of her age."

"Yackety-yack-yack!" Hans laughed as he led the way through the wood. "Follow me, Biddy. I'll soon have you home!"

6

The castle stood on the top of a high hill a short walk from the village.

"Be sure to arrive in good time," Biddy's mother warned, holding Tommy on her hip. "Be neat and tidy in everything you do."

The sun had just risen, the birds had begun to sing.

Pearl felt nervous as she put on her new

53

red cloak. "Mother, is the Duchess as bad-tempered as they say? Did she really kick the mothers down the stairs?"

"Ah, that sounds like one of Hans's tall stories!" her mother said lightly. "I never heard of it before."

But there was a false tone in her voice and an uneasy laugh as Pearl stepped out into the fresh morning air.

"Do as the Duchess tells you and all will be well," her mother insisted with a firm nudge to set Pearl on her way. "This is a good chance for you, Biddy. Please the Duchess and your fortune is made!"

"But she wants me to make her baby smile. What if I can't?"

"You will, my girl. Tell the baby nursery rhymes, sing to him and tickle him, make him laugh."

"I'll try," Pearl promised, looking ahead to the winding path up to the castle.

"Good girl. Remember – sing and tickle his toes. Now go!"

Pointed towers rose from each corner of the castle, almost reaching into the clouds. A hundred steps led up to the main doors.

"Eighty-three, eighty-four, eighty-five . . ." Pearl counted.

A light summer wind blew the hood back from her face.

The morning sun deepened the freckles on her face.

" . . . Ninety-seven, ninety-eight, ninety-nine, one hundred!" Pearl raised the golden lion-head knocker but before she had time to rap, the door opened and a man in a purple uniform and a white wig let her in.

"Who are you?" he asked rudely.

"I've come to look after the Duchess's baby," Pearl replied.

"In a *red* cloak?" the servant asked with disdain. "You have come to care for the Duchess's baby dressed in *red*!"

"What's wrong with that?"

The man raised his eyebrows and let her in. "The Duchess does not like red. She prefers purple, which she considers the most regal of colours. And gold."

Wow, did this Duchess like purple! As Pearl glanced around the big hallway she saw that the walls and ceilings were purple. There was a purple carpet on the floor. And yes – the curtains were purple too!

"Give me your cloak," the proud servant ordered. "Put on this apron."

Obediently Pearl tied the purple apron around her waist.

"Follow me to the nursery."

Up the golden stairs they went, along a golden corridor. "That is the Duke's room," the servant pointed out. "And that is the Duchess's. The room at the far end is the nursery."

"Wow!" Pearl gasped as the nursery door was opened. More purple walls and rugs, with a small golden cradle in the centre of the room.

"The baby is asleep," the servant said, preparing to leave. "The Duchess will arrive at noon to see if you have made him smile."

"Wait!" Pearl pleaded. "Are there any toys – teddy bears or rattles that might help?"

Up went the servant's eyebrows again. "Toys?"

"I guess that's a 'no'," Pearl muttered, tiptoeing towards the cradle. "Wish me luck," she said as a parting shot.

For the first time the man dropped his proud act. "You'll need more than luck," he confided.

"How come?" Pearl asked, scared even to look at the grumpy baby.

"You're the third girl this week to try to make him smile," came the plain answer. "First Helena, then Marie, now you."

"W-w-what happened to Helena and Marie?" Pearl asked, more nervous than ever.

"They tried and tried but there was no glimmer of a smile. The Duchess had them—"

"Kicked downstairs?" Pearl asked in a hoarse whisper.

"Worse!"

"She had them locked in the dungeons?"

"Guess again."

"Thrown to the wolves?" Pearl gasped.

"Correct!" the man said, closing the nursery door with a loud click.

7

Pearl tiptoed up to the golden crib. The baby was wrapped in a white blanket, sleeping soundly. He had golden curls and a round face. *Just like Tommy*, she thought. *He looks the same as any other baby, so how hard can this be?*

She wondered if she should wake him and make him play. *No, better not.* Instead, she wandered to the window and looked down on the wooded hillside. In the far distance the river ran through the valley like a shining silver ribbon. She heard a blast from a huntsman's horn and caught sight of three riders galloping across the hill, chasing a stag.

"Poor deer," she murmured. "I hope they don't catch you."

Another loud blast from the horn made the baby stir in his crib. Pearl dashed to be with him.

"Erhhhh!" Baby whimpered as he opened his big blue eyes.

"Shush! There, there!" She rocked the cradle to calm him.

"Werrhhh!" he grizzled. He stared up at Pearl.

"OK, let me lift you up," Pearl said, taking him out of the crib. He was warm and heavy, with tiny plump pink fingers and toes. "What shall we play?"

"Waargghh!" Baby opened his mouth and bawled.

"Shush!" Pearl begged, rocking him and pacing the room. "Don't cry. Come on, let's play 'Round and Round the Garden'."

She opened his tiny palm and tickled it as she chanted the rhyme. "'Round and round the garden, Like a teddy bear . . .'"

Baby stopped crying and looked interested.

"'One step, two steps . . . Tickly under there!'"

Baby gasped then made a gurgling sound. Not quite a giggle, but definitely not a cry.

"Again?" Pearl asked.

"Nyah!"

"Yes? OK. Now this time, please smile! 'Round and round the garden . . .'"

"Not bad!" The proud servant popped his head round the door just before noon. "I only heard Baby cry once. Well done."

"Thanks." Pearl was worn out with the rhymes and the games, the tickling and the jiggling up and down. Looking after Baby was hard work. "Come and see. Do you think he's smiling?"

The servant inspected Baby's round face. "There's a dimple on one cheek and a sparkle in his eyes. Yes, I'd say that is most definitely a smile!"

"Phew!" At the sound of the huntsmen returning to the castle, Pearl carried the baby to the window. She showed him the trees and the river far below.

In the courtyard, horses neighed, voices shouted and doors slammed.

"Waarrgghhhh!" The sudden noise startled Baby.

"Oops!" Pearl carried him away from the window but it was too late.

"Waagh! Waagh! Waagh!"

Just then the nursery door flew open and the Purple Duchess dashed in. "Foolish girl!" she cried. "Your task is to make him smile, not to scare him out of his wits!"

"I didn't . . . I wasn't . . ." Pearl stammered. She turned to the servant. "He was smiling just now, wasn't he?"

The servant looked down at his feet and coughed awkwardly.

"He was – really!" Pearl protested. "We've played games. He loves 'Round and Round the Garden'!"

"Here, let me have him!" The Duchess whisked Baby away, calling for nursemaids and sentries.

A small army of women carrying feeding-bottles and teething-rings ran down the corridor into the room. Two men with spears soon followed.

"Take him. Feed him. Walk him in the fresh air!" the Purple Duchess ordered the nursemaids.

"Wrrraaaaggghhhh!" Baby screeched as he was carried away.

"And take this foolish girl into the forest!" the Duchess raged. She was in an especially bad mood because her husband, the Duke, had let the stag escape and now there would be no roast venison for supper. "Leave her in the darkest thicket and let the wolves have her!"

"No, please!" Pearl begged the sentries.

They lifted her off her feet and rushed her out of the nursery, past the spiteful Duchess. Down the purple corridor, down the stairs, across the hallway, until the proud servant caught up with them to hand Pearl her red cloak.

"Here!" he said.

The sentries threw open the doors, ready to thrust Pearl into the forest.

"Listen to me!" the servant whispered in a low voice. "It's not as bad as you think. You will not get lost if you listen to the wise owl!"

Struggling to catch her breath, Pearl nodded.

"Ask the owl to show you the way home!" the servant insisted.

Then the sentries seized her again and carried her deep into the forest.

8

"Whoo-whoo, take care. Look to your left!" the owl hooted.

Pearl felt there were eyes watching her, footsteps following her. Everywhere she looked there was danger.

The owl flew slowly ahead like a white ghost in the darkness. "Dooo not be afraid!" he called. "Take courage and follooow me!"

With her heart in her mouth, Pearl stumbled down the hillside. Overhead the trees sighed in the wind.

In the undergrowth the Wolf prowled. His breath was hot, his eyes gleaming. *The owl will not save Little Red Riding-Hood! My jaws are strong. My teeth are sharp.*

Pearl saw the owl alight on a branch. He looked down at her with enormous, bright eyes. "Pick up a stout stick," he told her. "Use it as a weapon to beat off the enemy."

So Pearl found a stick. "How far is it until we reach the edge of the forest?"

"Can yoooou hear the waterfall crashing over the rocks?"

She nodded.

"That is the edge of the forest. Looook ahead. Follow the sound of the water, whoo-whoo!"

She will slip and fall. I will pounce! the Wolf thought.

A deer sprang out of the bushes and raced ahead of Pearl and the owl. "The Wolf is watching you," the deer whispered, her eyes startled, her long legs leaping. "Be ready to fight him off!"

"Onwards!" the owl insisted as the deer leaped out of sight.

Pearl struggled on. She leaned on the stick as the way grew steep and the grass grew wet and slippy.

Hip-hop – a big green frog flopped on to a flat rock. "The Wolf is close by!" he croaked. "Do not rest until you are out of the forest!"

Thump-thump went Pearl's heart. Her red cloak caught on a thorn bush but she tore it free. She slipped on the rocks and began to slide.

Now! thought the Wolf, crouching low.

"Help!" Pearl cried. She lost her stick as she fell into the stream that rushed towards the crashing waterfall.

Then the sunlight hit her and the cold water sparkled. She was out of the forest, being swept downstream. The Wolf was racing along the bank beside her, his jaws snapping, but afraid to plunge into the foaming torrent.

Pearl's red cloak billowed out across the stream. She sped under low branches, the water whirling her against the bank. The edge of the waterfall was only a few steps away.

"Reach out!" a voice cried from the bank.

The Wolf stopped and snarled.

Pearl stretched out and grabbed a hand.

She felt herself heaved out of the stream. "You again!" she said to Hans.

"Yes, me again." He pulled her on to dry land. "Someone has to look out for you when you go to the castle, Little Red Riding-Hood!"

Snarling, the Wolf crept forward. *Two for the price of one!* he thought recklessly.

The owl flapped his wings and flew off with a loud whit-tu-whoo.

"What happened? Did the Duchess throw you out?" Hans asked Pearl.

She nodded then took a good look round. "Watch out. The animals say there's a wolf nearby."

Right here! Wolfie thought, creeping closer. *Under your noses, ready to pounce!*

"Run!" the rabbits said, scurrying up the

hill into their burrow. Their white tails bobbed out of sight.

"Right now – run!" a frog croaked, plopping into the stream.

"I'm not scared of Mister Wolf!" Hans declared in a loud voice.

"Well, I am!" Pearl admitted. She didn't know where to turn, which way to run.

But Hans seized his woodcutter's axe which he'd leaned against a tree. He saw a pair of yellow eyes gleaming from behind the nearest rock. "Come out, Wolfie – I dare you!"

The Wolf's eyes glinted, his jaws snapped. He stared at the sharp blade of Hans's axe.

Pearl saw the Wolf at last. He was big and grey and furry, with a long bushy tail.

His lips were curled back in a snarl. "Here's a taste of your own medicine!" Hans yelled, raising the axe and jumping on to the rock.

Wolfie reared back as Hans swung the axe. The blade nicked the tip of his tail and he howled. *Aawoooo!*

"Got you!" Hans cried. "How do you like that?"

At this the Wolf turned. He crashed away through the bushes, blundering into trees and tripping over rocks.

*

Soon he was gone.

And Hans and Pearl scrambled down the sunny hillside until they reached the river. Their village lay ahead at the edge of the flower meadow where the cows grazed.

"Well done, Hans," they said, calmly raising their heavy heads as Pearl and Hans passed by. *Chew-chew.* "You are the brave hero who saved Little Red Riding-Hood from the Wolf!"

9

Rat-a-tat-tat! There was a loud knock at the cottage door early next morning.

"Answer that while I feed Tommy his breakfast," Little Red Riding-Hood's mother said.

Pearl opened the door to find Hans leaning cockily against the doorpost. "Ah, my hero!" she grinned.

"Yeah, that's me. Your very own knight

in shining armour!"

Pearl wrinkled her nose at his leather shorts and thick woollen socks. "You're so not!" she laughed.

"Hey, it's true! I saved you from Mister Wolf, didn't I?"

"Shh! Mum doesn't know." Pearl had explained away her wet clothes by saying she'd slipped in the stream. After all, why make her mum worry about wolves when she had a baby to feed and a hundred and one jobs to do?

"Did you tell her the Duchess kicked you out?"

Pearl nodded. "She was a bit upset that I only lasted a day. But she says at least it means I can go and visit Grandma again today. Miller Thompson rode by on his way to market and told us she was sick."

Hans frowned. "Listen, I won't be around to look after you today. That's what I came to tell you – I have to go to the market with Dad."

"Tuttt!" Pearl tossed her head. "I don't need you to look after me *every* day!"

"Says you!"

"It's true. I can take care of myself." Pearl felt she was getting used to life in Red Riding Hood world. And now that she knew the quickest way through the wood, she planned to head straight to her grandmother's house and straight back again.

"No daydreaming," Hans warned.

"OK, and no tricks or jokes from you either."

"Me?" He spread his hands, palms upwards. "Listen, I have to hurry. Say hello to your grandmamma from me!"

And with that, Hans jumped on to the back of his dad's cart, and father and son set off for market.

"Your grandmamma always likes a nice rice pudding," Red Riding-Hood's mother said as she packed the basket. "Be sure to tell her it's made with plenty of sugar and . . ."

"Milk from Daisy," Pearl guessed.

"Yes. And be sure she knows there's a jar of candied lemon in the bottom of the basket, and a pot of honey from the hive in our back garden." Telling Pearl to put on her cloak, she hurried her daughter out of the cottage door.

Pearl put the basket over her arm and stepped out smartly across the meadow.

"Good morning, Little Red-Riding Hood!" the cows said sweetly. "We hope you enjoy the bright, sunny day!"

"I will," Pearl replied, walking on briskly.

Soon she came to the stile that led into the wood.

"Take care," two grey doves cooed from the branch of a tree. "Be sure not to leave the path!"

"I will," Pearl promised. All seemed happy and peaceful. Baby rabbits played on the path ahead, a squirrel ran up a tree trunk, chattering noisily.

But then the peace was broken by the sound of the Duke's hunting horn and the sight of half a dozen riders galloping through the wood. Suddenly all the animals took flight, leaving Pearl rooted to the spot.

"Ride on, ride on!" The Duke was in his hunting cloak of fur and velvet. He wore a velvet hat with a tall feather. His men

charged through the wood after him. "The stag has fled down from the mountain and across the meadow, in fear of his life. Onwards, men – on!"

They rode past Pearl, close enough for her to see the sweat on their horses' flanks and fear in their eyes as their riders spurred them. Swerving round trees, they galloped on.

The Duke is as bad as the Duchess! Pearl thought as calm returned to the wood

once more. *But at least they'll have scared Wolfie off if he happened to be lurking in the bushes.*

Eyes wide, and holding her breath, she took a good look around. It was true – there wasn't an animal anywhere in sight. In the distance, the huntsmen blew their horn.

But then there was a rustle in the dark shadows on the path ahead. Then the snap of a twig. *Huh!* "Who's there?" Pearl called. She held her basket of food close to her chest and walked on warily.

Another rustle. Another snap.

"Hans, is that you? Are you playing one of your tricks?"

Silence.

Pearl paused and stared into the

shadows. "Hans, if it is you, I'm really cross this time!"

She took one step forward, then another. She was certain there was a creature in the thicket to one side of the path – a definite sense of something alive and hiding.

Better grab a weapon! Pearl thought. It seemed Wolfie just didn't give up. So she picked up a hefty stick and inched forward.

"Do not be afraid," a soft voice said from the thicket.

"Who are you? Who's there?" Pearl gasped. She stepped towards the tangle of undergrowth.

"I am too weak to go on," the creature said. "The Duke and his men have hunted me close to death."

Now Pearl made out a pair of mighty antlers. "You're the stag!" she whispered, overcome with wonder.

"The men almost ran me down," he sighed. He was a tall creature with a broad white chest and a noble head. "They call me the king of the forest, but my strength has gone."

"You're OK?" Pearl asked anxiously. "They didn't hurt you?"

"I am not injured," the stag replied in his deep voice. "I will rest a while then return to the mountain."

"Good. And the Duke is miles

away by now. They galloped off in the other direction. You can take your time."

"And you, child?" the stag asked, looking kindly at Pearl. "They did not harm you?"

She shook her head. "I was scared to death as usual. But I'm fine."

"Good. Then I will rest and you will continue your journey."

"To my grandmother's house," Pearl explained. "I'm supposed to hurry straight there and back again."

"Then go," the stag said, his antlered head raised high. "Do not linger. Farewell."

10

There was no wind in the windmill's sails as Pearl walked by, and no sign of life outside her grandmother's house.

"Hello?" Pearl knocked on the door and opened it.

Tilly the striped cat strolled towards her, brushing against her legs then wandering outside.

"Grandmamma, are you in bed?" Pearl

asked. She put her basket on the table and tiptoed upstairs. She knocked on the bedroom door.

There was no reply.

"Are you asleep?" Pearl listened through the door. "Grandmamma, can I come in?"

Still no one answered.

This is not good! Pearl thought. Perhaps her grandmother was too ill to speak. Gently she opened the door and looked into the bedroom.

The bed was empty.

"Oh no!" Pearl gasped. Straight away she thought the worst – that Wolfie had got here first and pounced on the helpless old woman. He'd dragged her off into the wood, and her grandmamma would never be seen again!

"Grandma!" Pearl dashed downstairs and flew out of the cottage in such haste that she almost tripped over Tilly, who was sunning herself on the doorstep.

"Watch where you're going," the cat complained in a high voice. She jumped on to the windowsill and shook her head. "You can shout as loud as you like, Little Red Riding-Hood, but she won't hear you."

"Why, what happened to her?" Pearl gasped. "Was it Wolfie? Did he get her?"

"Calm down, dear," Tilly insisted.

 "What's this nonsense about a wolf? Speak plainly."

"Grandmamma's not in her bed – she's supposed to

90

be ill. Where is she?"

"Ah!" Tilly opened her mouth and yawned. "She was perhaps a little poorly during the night, but she got up after the miller set off for market and had porridge for breakfast. After that she felt better."

"And?" Pearl prompted.

"Let me see." The cat took her time. "Ah yes, after that, she swept and dusted the house. Then she watered the flowers in the pots by the door."

"No, I mean – where is she now?"

Tilly blinked. "I believe she's out collecting wild strawberries for jam. She won't be back until midday."

"Right." Pearl gave a sigh of relief. "That's OK then. Sorry I panicked."

"Don't worry, my dear." Jumping down

from the windowsill, Tilly strolled into the kitchen and took a sniff at Pearl's basket.

"Mmmm – I smell your mother's best rice pudding!" she purred.

There was no point waiting for her grandmother until midday, Pearl decided. So she gave Tilly a spoonful of rice pudding and left a note for her grandmother.

"Dear Grandmamma, I'm glad you're feeling better. Mum sent me over with a few treats. I hope you like them. Love, Little Red Riding-Hood."

Then she set off with the empty basket, past the deserted mill and into the woods.

"La-la-la, dah-di-dah!" Pearl sang. She did a little skip in her neat red clogs. Then she swished her cloak and pretended she was Superman twirling into his costume and flying through the air. "Da-da-dah-du-dah!"

She didn't notice that there were no squirrels or rabbits playing happily, or that the wood was eerily quiet – not until she came to the woodcutter's clearing and paused to look around.

"Where is everybody?" she said out loud. Then she remembered that Hans and his dad were at the market, and thought perhaps that the woodland animals needed a midday rest. *Like me*, she thought, sitting on a log.

Not far away, the Wolf was on the prowl. Twice he'd tried to pounce on Little Red Riding-Hood and twice he'd failed. *Third time lucky!* he thought.

He padded silently under the trees while the squirrels scrambled high in the branches and the rabbits took to their burrows. Then he stopped to lift his head and sniff the air.

Pearl felt weary but she knew she must carry on. So she stood up and began to walk across the clearing.

And what luck! Wolfie thought as he spied the red cloak. *She is alone and helpless. I will have her for my dinner!*

Closer he crept as Pearl headed for home. He didn't make a sound except for the rapid panting of his breath.

"That's weird!" Pearl said, stopping. "I suddenly felt cold."

"Tu-whoo, turn around!" the owl said from high above, but he couldn't make Pearl hear.

"Is anybody there?" she asked. Her voice sounded small and hollow.

Me! Wolfie sprang out from behind a tree. His teeth flashed, his yellow eyes glared.

Pearl turned and gasped. She flung herself sideways as Wolfie pounced.

Rolling down a short slope, she picked herself up and ran back into the clearing, trying to reach the far side, where a woodcutter's axe leaned against a tree.

The Wolf snarled and lunged after her. "There is no escape!" he cried.

Pearl's heart was in her mouth, she could hardly breathe. But she saw a tree straight ahead that was easy to climb and she seized her chance, grabbing the lowest branch and swinging herself up out of the Wolf's reach.

Wolfie screeched to a halt below. He gnashed his teeth and snarled.

Though her legs trembled and her hands shook, Pearl made it up to a second branch then a third. Surely Wolfie wouldn't be able to follow her now.

"Hah!" the Wolf said, prowling below. His savage mouth seemed to smile. "How long do you think you can stay up there?"

"For ever!" Pearl swore, holding tight as the tree swayed. Her stomach lurched and she swallowed hard.

"I doubt it," Wolfie sneered. "The wind will blow you down. The branch will break. You will be mine!"

"Agh!" Pearl yelled as, sure enough, the wind blew harder and the branch she was sitting on began to creak. Desperate, she stared down at Wolfie's savage jaws.

Creak, then *crack*! The thin branch gave way.

Pearl plunged to the ground, her cloak flying from her shoulders as she fell.

Thump! She hit the ground and rolled. The red cloak fell on to the Wolf, covering him completely. He snarled and struggled beneath it.

"Right!" Pearl said, finding her courage and turning to seize the axe Hans's dad had left by the tree. By the time Wolfie had crawled out from under the cloak, Pearl stood with the axe raised above her head. "If you take one step nearer, I'll use it!"

The Wolf bared his fangs. The hair on his neck stood on end. "Fine words!" he snarled.

"If you don't believe me, try this!" Pearl yelled. She brought the axe down so close to Wolfie that it snipped another little piece off his tail.

"Aawooo!" he howled.

"And this!" Pearl cried. Who needed Hans when she could *chop-chop-chop* with the axe?

The Wolf jumped this way and that to escape the shiny blade. At last he broke free.

"No dinner for you tonight, you chicken!" Pearl called after him. Wolfie was scared and it served him right.

From a safe distance the Wolf narrowed his wicked eyes. "Perhaps not tonight," he snarled, turning to slink off into the wood. "But tomorrow, Red Riding-Hood, or the day after . . . I promise I'll be back!"

11

"Go on, beat it!" Pearl yelled. She waved the axe and watched Wolfie flee. She marched on home with a spring in her step.

"Why are you looking like the cat that got the cream?" Hans asked suspiciously. He'd just got back from market and was unloading carrots and potatoes from the cart.

"Because I beat Mister Wolf at his own game!" Pearl beamed. "Thanks to your dad's sharp axe. And this red cloak came in very handy, I can tell you!"

"How was your grandmother?" Little Red Riding-Hood's mother asked, up to her elbows in soapsuds. She was washing Tommy's clothes while he slept.

"Better!" Pearl reported. "In fact, she was out, so I left her a note."

"Good. Well, sit down at the table and rest. You'll see I've baked a cake."

"Mmmm, ginger!" Hungry after her adventure, Pearl took a big slice from the plate and bit into it.

As she swallowed, a warm wind blew in through the door. It caught the soap suds

and lifted shiny bubbles from the sink. They drifted towards Pearl, grew brighter and then popped. *Pop! Pop! Pop!* A white light surrounded her.

"Whoo, I'm feeling dizzy again!" Pearl gasped.

Then, the room began to spin – round and round. Bubbles popped and the glittering light lifted her. Soon Pearl floated out of the cottage, up and up into the bright blue sky.

"Pearl is never coming back!" Lily groaned in the basement of Amber's house. She sat on the floor beside the dressing-up box.

Amber took off her cat mask and sighed. "If she went into Hansel and Gretel world, I bet the red-eyed witch got her."

"She's probably lost in some deep, dark forest, starving to death!" Lily pushed to one side the piece of ginger cake which Amber's mum had given her.

"Or worse!" Amber groaned.

But then the room filled with bright

light and with a whoosh, Pearl was back.

"Oh, you poor thing!" Lily cried, rushing towards her.

"What was it like? Did the witch get you?" Amber asked.

"Hey, don't crowd me!" Pearl said. Her head was still in a whirl as she pushed back the hood of her bright red cloak.

"Poor you!" Amber sighed. "I'm sorry it didn't work out for you, Pearl, I really am."

"What do you mean – it didn't work out?" Pearl felt as if she was walking on air. She clicked her clogs and did a little dance. "I might not be a princess, but actually, it was great!"

"B-b-but . . .!" Amber and Lily both stammered.

"I lived in a cute cottage at the edge of the wood. There are flowers growing everywhere, and the animals *talk*!"

"Whoa!" Amber said.

"Which animals? Where?" Lily asked.

"Everywhere! The cows moo and say hello when I walk to my grandmother's house. The owl shows me the way. And you should have heard the stag's voice – so deep!"

Amber and Lily stared at Pearl as she gabbled on.

"The Duke and Duchess live in a castle on the hill, and they're well mean. There's a boy called Hans who lives next door, and he's a bit annoying. But his dad's a woodcutter and Hans is OK really, if you don't count his stupid leather shorts. And guess what – I beat Wolfie! All by myself. I didn't need anyone to help me."

"Wolfie?" Lily and Amber echoed.

"Yes, you know – the big bad Wolf who tries to eat me up!"

"What about the witch?" Amber asked.

"What about Hansel, and all that stuff with the gingerbread house?" Lily wanted to know. "What was it like being Gretel?"

Pearl laughed. "That's not who I was, silly!"

"Aah!" Amber tugged at Pearl's long cloak. "Wolf. Grandmamma. Woodcutter!"

"Exactly!" Pearl grinned. "I'm Little Red Riding-Hood. And I had the *best* time!"

Have you checked out...

www.dressingupdreams.net

It's the place to go for games, downloads, activities, sneak previews and lots of fun!

You'll find a special dressing-up game and lots of activities and fun things to do, as well as news on Dressing-Up Dreams and all your favourite characters.

Sign up to the newsletter at **www.dressingupdreams.net** to receive extra clothes for your Dressing-Up Dreams doll and the opportunity to enter special members only competitions.

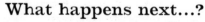

What happens next...?
Log onto www.dressingupdreams.net for a sneak preview of my next adventure!

WIN A *Dressing-Up Dreams* GOODIE BAG!

CAN YOU SPOT THE TWO DIFFERENCES AND THE HIDDEN LETTER IN THESE TWO PICTURES OF PEARL?

There is a spot-the-difference picture and hidden letter in the back of all four
Dressing-Up Dreams books about Pearl (look for the books with
9 to 12 on the spine). Hidden in one of the pictures above is a secret letter.
Find all four letters and put them together to make a special Dressing-Up
Dreams word, then send it to us. Each month, we will put the correct entries
in a draw and one lucky winner will receive a magical Dressing-Up Dreams
goodie bag including an exclusive Dressing-Up Dreams keyring!

Send your magical word, your name, age and your address
on a postcard to: **Pearl's Dressing-Up Dreams Competition**

UK Readers:
Hodder Children's Books
338 Euston Road
London NW1 3BH
dsmarketing@hodder.co.uk

Australian Readers:
Hachette Children's Books
Level 17/207 Kent Street
Sydney NSW 2000
childrens.books@hachette.com.au

New Zealand Readers:
Hachette Livre NZ Ltd
PO Box 100 749
North Shore City 0745
childrensbooks@hachette.co.nz

Only one entry per child. Final draw: 30th March 2010
For full terms and conditions go to http://www.hodderchildrens.co.uk/Terms_and_Conditions.htm

COLOURING FUN!

Carefully colour the Dressing-Up Dreams picture on the next page and then send it in to us.

Or you can draw your very own fairytale character. You might want to think about what they would wear or if they have special powers.

Each month, we will put the best entries on the website gallery and one lucky winner will receive a magical Dressing-Up Dreams goodie bag!

Send your drawing,
your name, age and address on a postcard to:
Pearl's Dressing-Up Dreams Competition

UK Readers:
Hodder Children's Books
338 Euston Road
London NW1 3BH
kidsmarketing@hodder.co.uk

Australian Readers:
Hachette Children's Books
Level 17/207 Kent Street
Sydney NSW 2000
childrens.books@hachette.com.au

New Zealand Readers:
Hachette Livre NZ Ltd
PO Box 100 749
North Shore City 0745
childrensbooks@hachette.co.